MARVEL
CAPTAIN MARVEL

By John Sazaklis
Illustrated by Penelope R. Gaylord

 A GOLDEN BOOK · NEW YORK

MARVEL © 2019 MARVEL

All rights reserved. Published in the United States by Golden Books, an imprint of Random House Children's Books, a division of Penguin Random House LLC, 1745 Broadway, New York, NY 10019, and in Canada by Penguin Random House Canada Limited, Toronto. Golden Books, A Golden Book, A Little Golden Book, the G colophon, and the distinctive gold spine are registered trademarks of Penguin Random House LLC.

rhcbooks.com

Educators and librarians, for a variety of teaching tools, visit us at RHTeachersLibrarians.com

ISBN 978-0-5247-6870-6 (trade) — ISBN 978-1-5247-6871-3 (ebook)

Printed in the United States of America

10 9 8 7 6 5 4 3 2 1

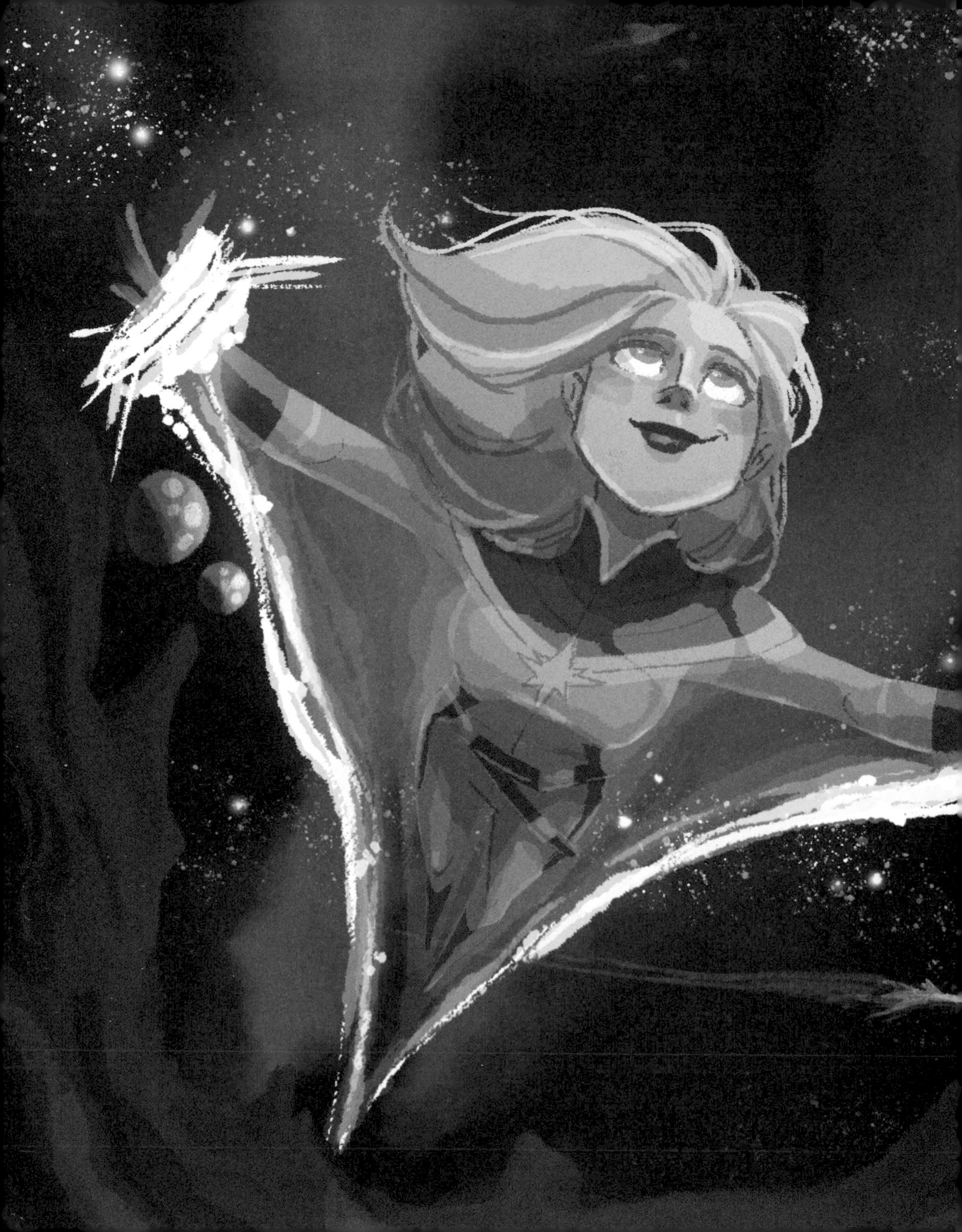

CAPTAIN MARVEL is an interstellar Super Hero. She protects all planets in the galaxy—especially her home planet, Earth!

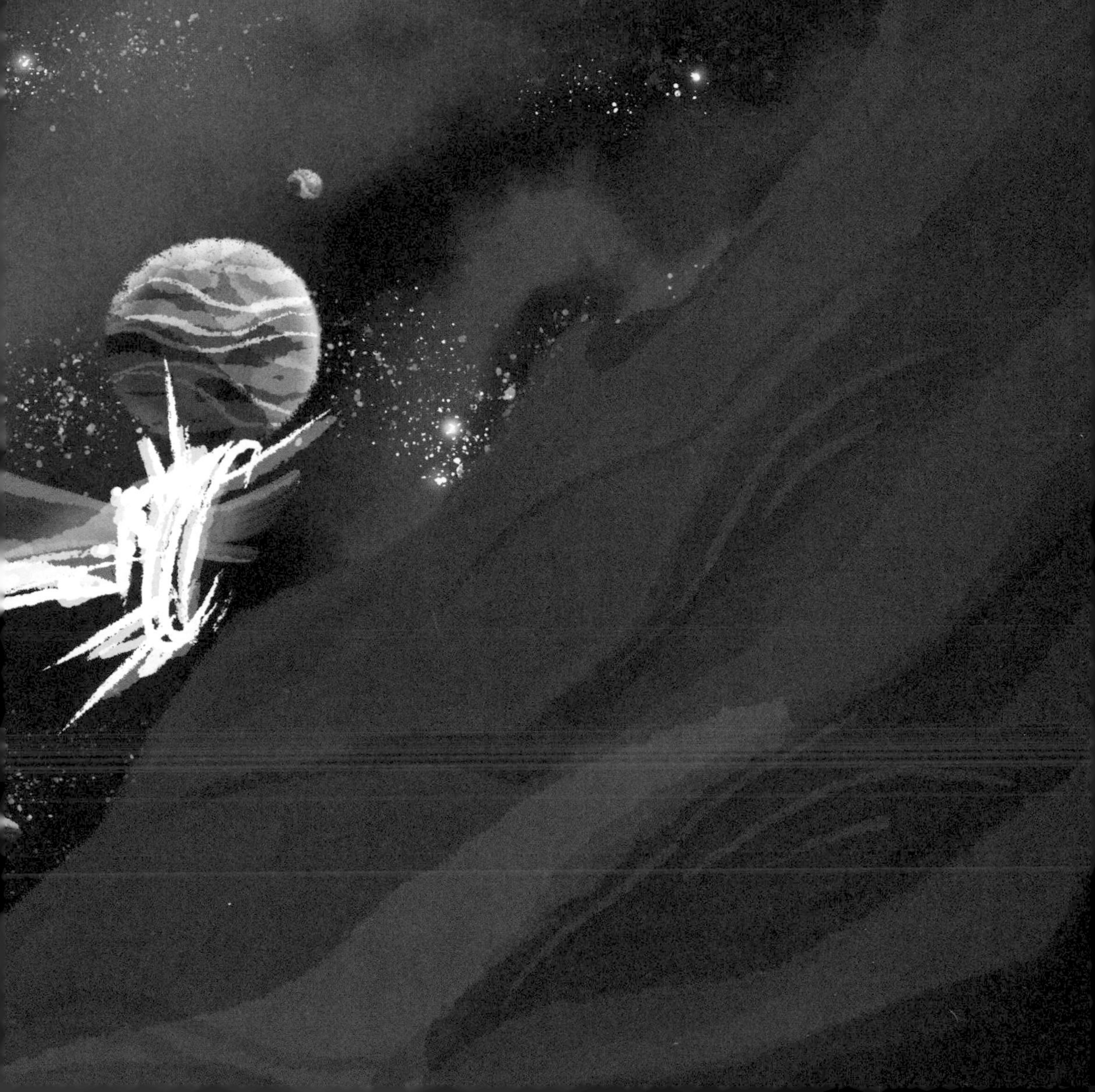

Captain Marvel is really Carol Danvers.
She was once an air force captain.
She could **FLY** higher . . .

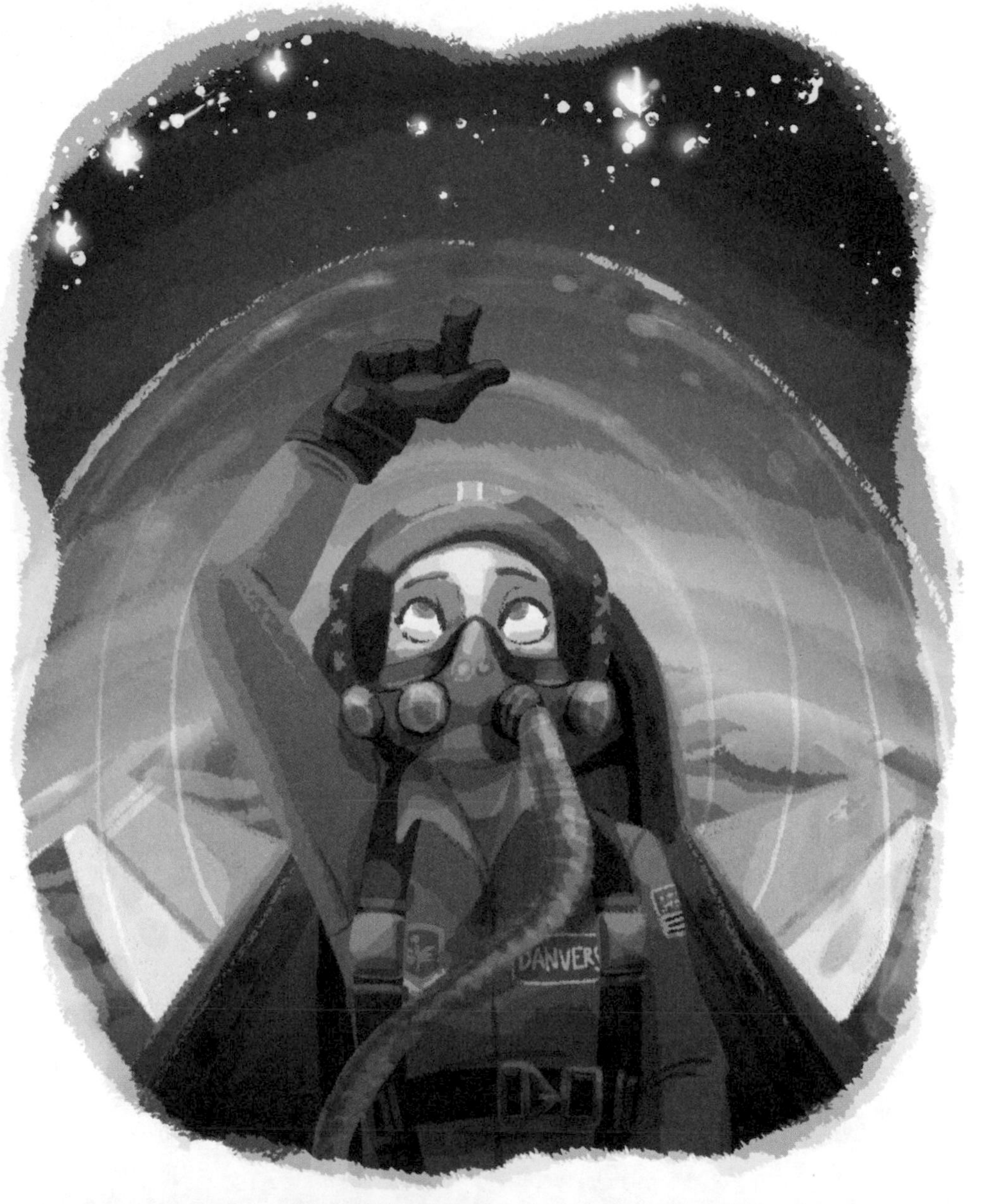
DANVERS

. . . and **FASTER**
than any other pilot!

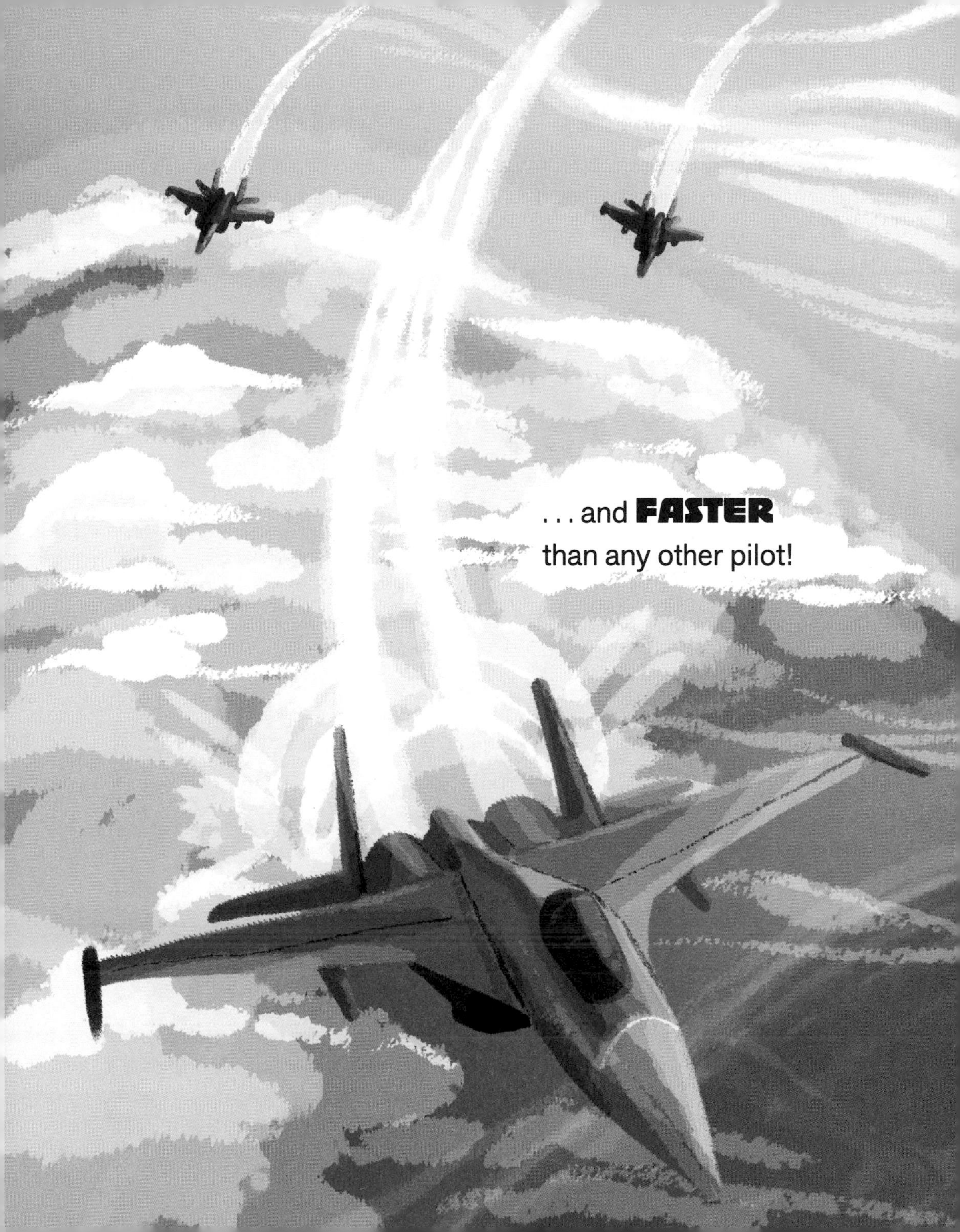

Carol Danvers even went on secret missions in outer space. She once caught an alien spy stealing a mysterious device.

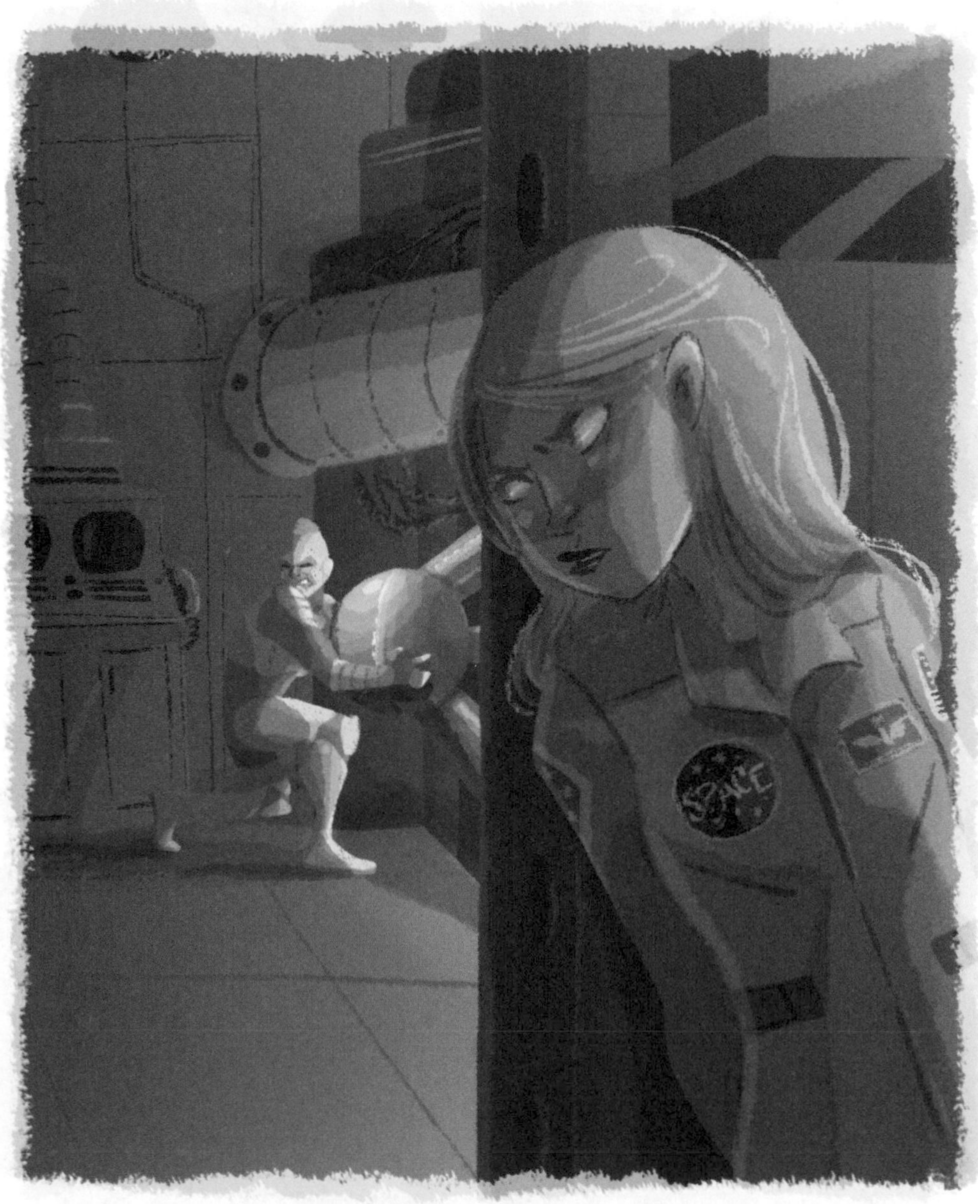
SPACE

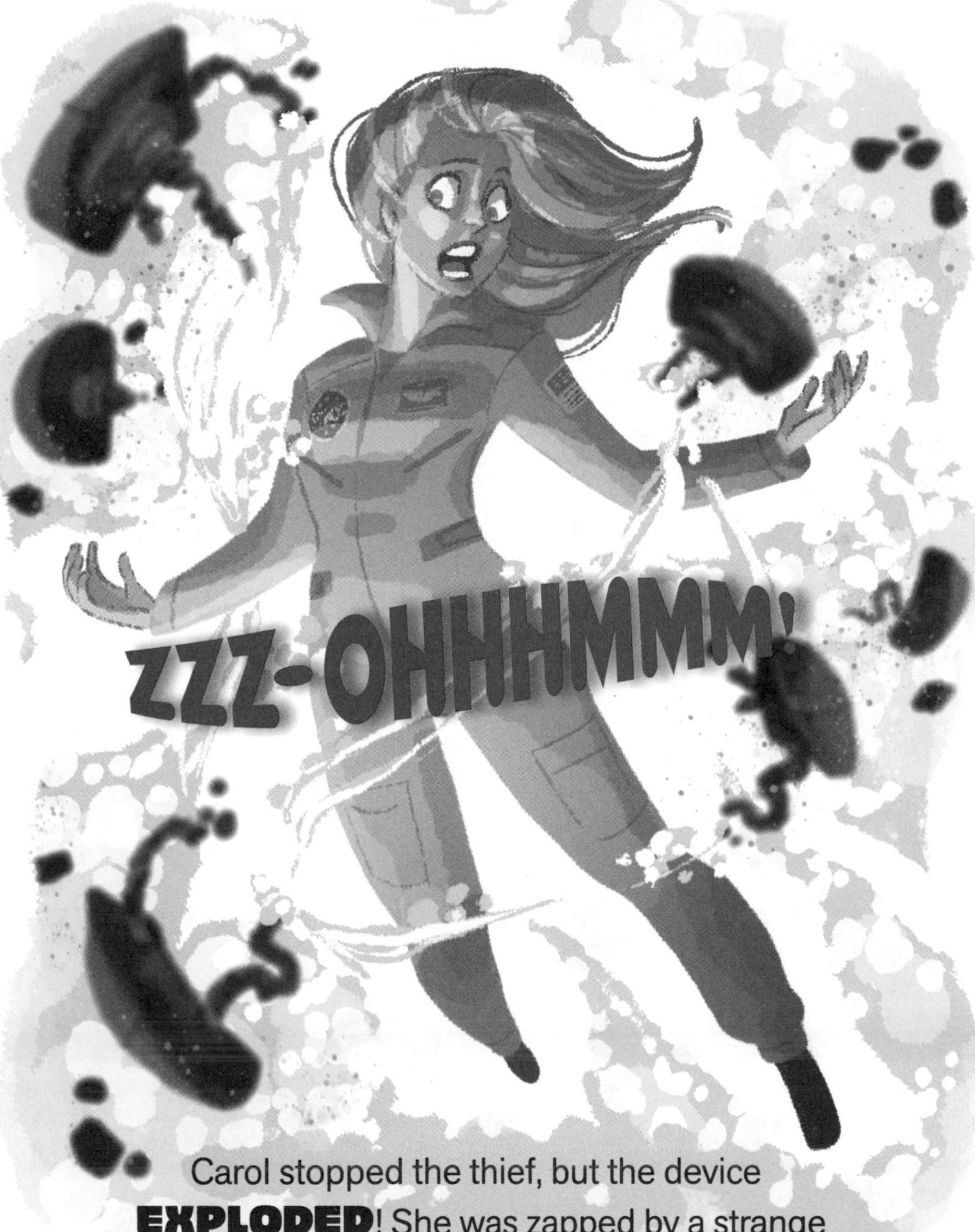
ZZZ-OHHHMMMM!

Carol stopped the thief, but the device **EXPLODED**! She was zapped by a strange energy that gave her special abilities.

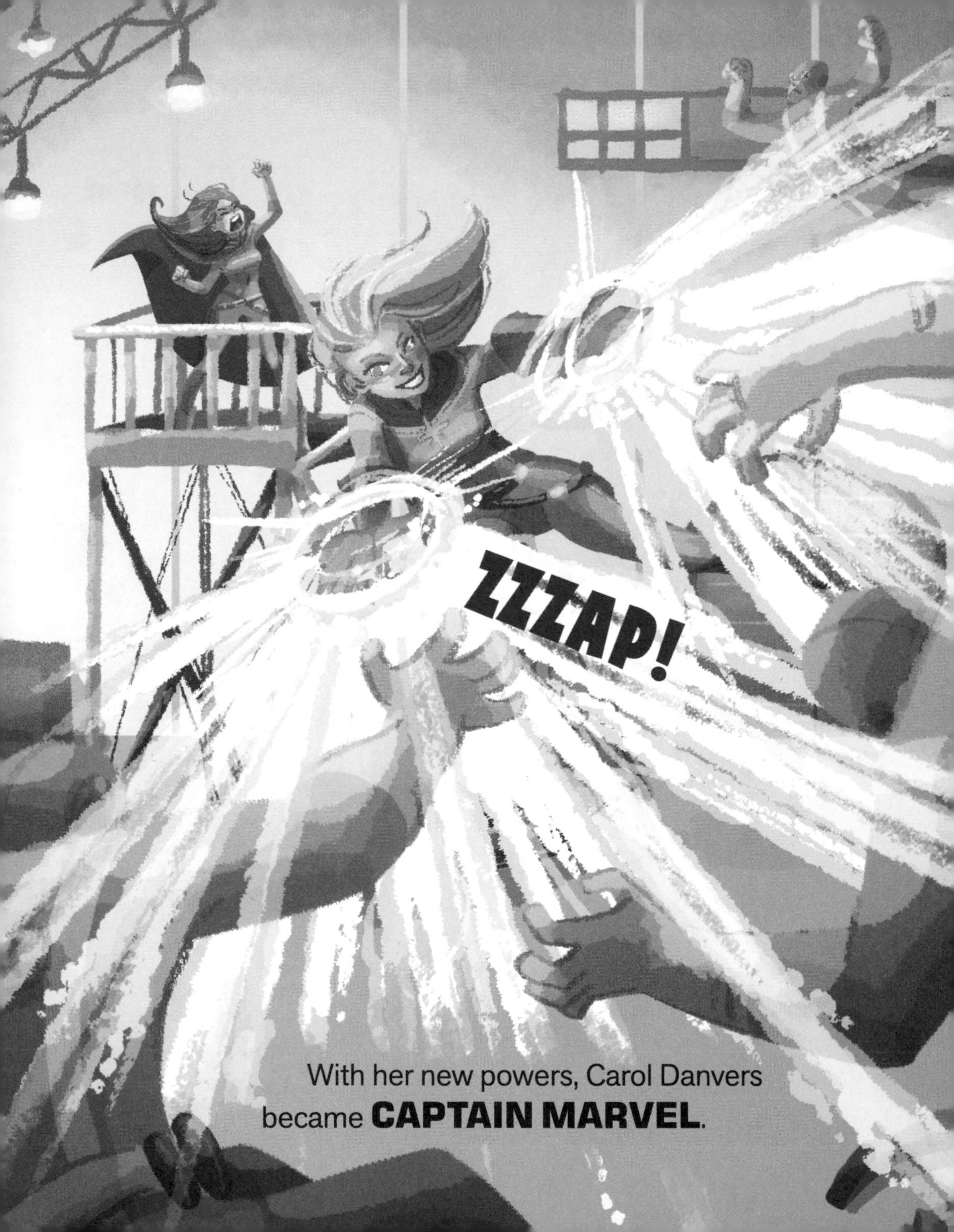
ZZZAP!

With her new powers, Carol Danvers
became **CAPTAIN MARVEL**.

She can fly—and fire energy beams from her hands!

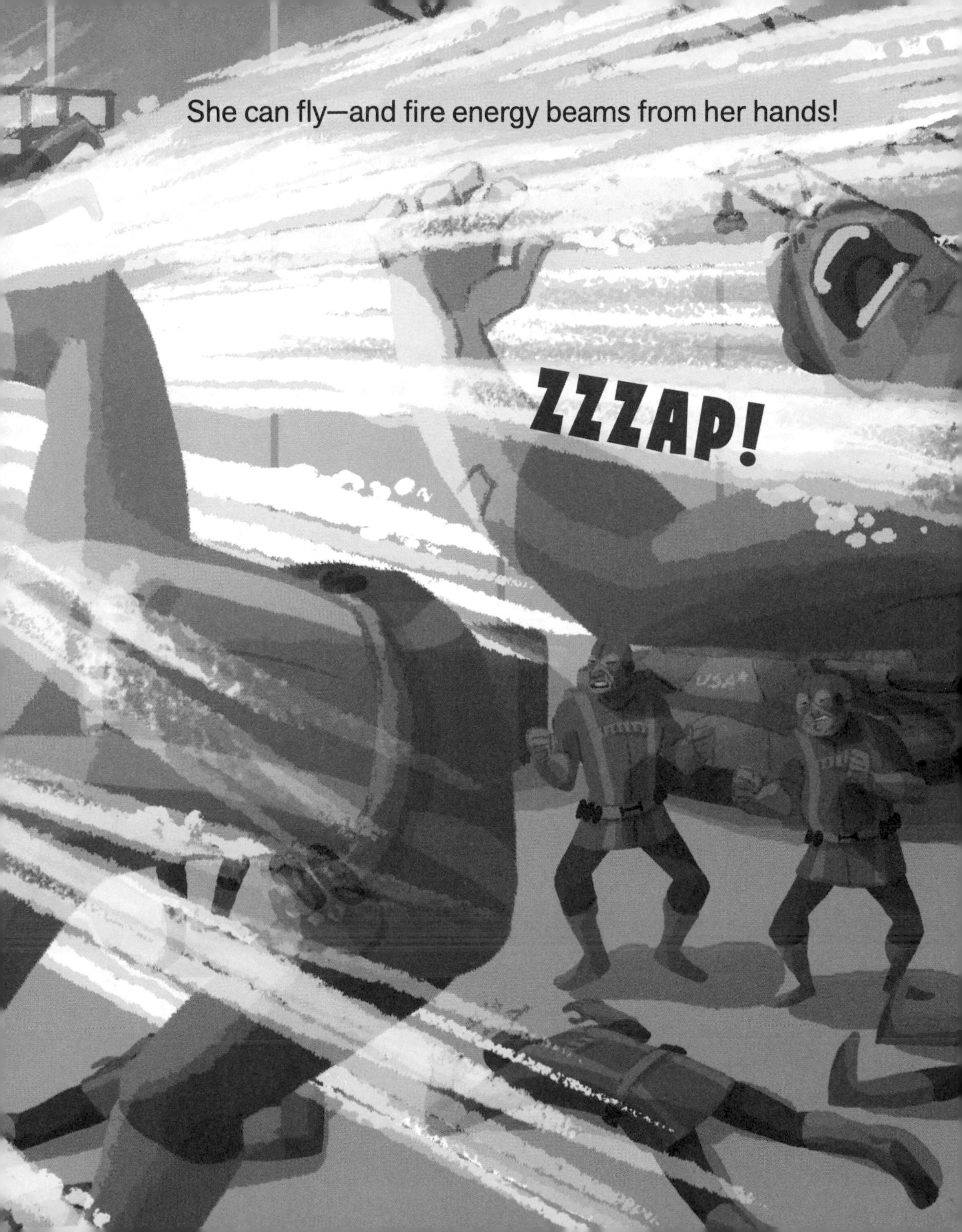
ZZZAP!

Captain Marvel is **INCREDIBLY FAST** . . .

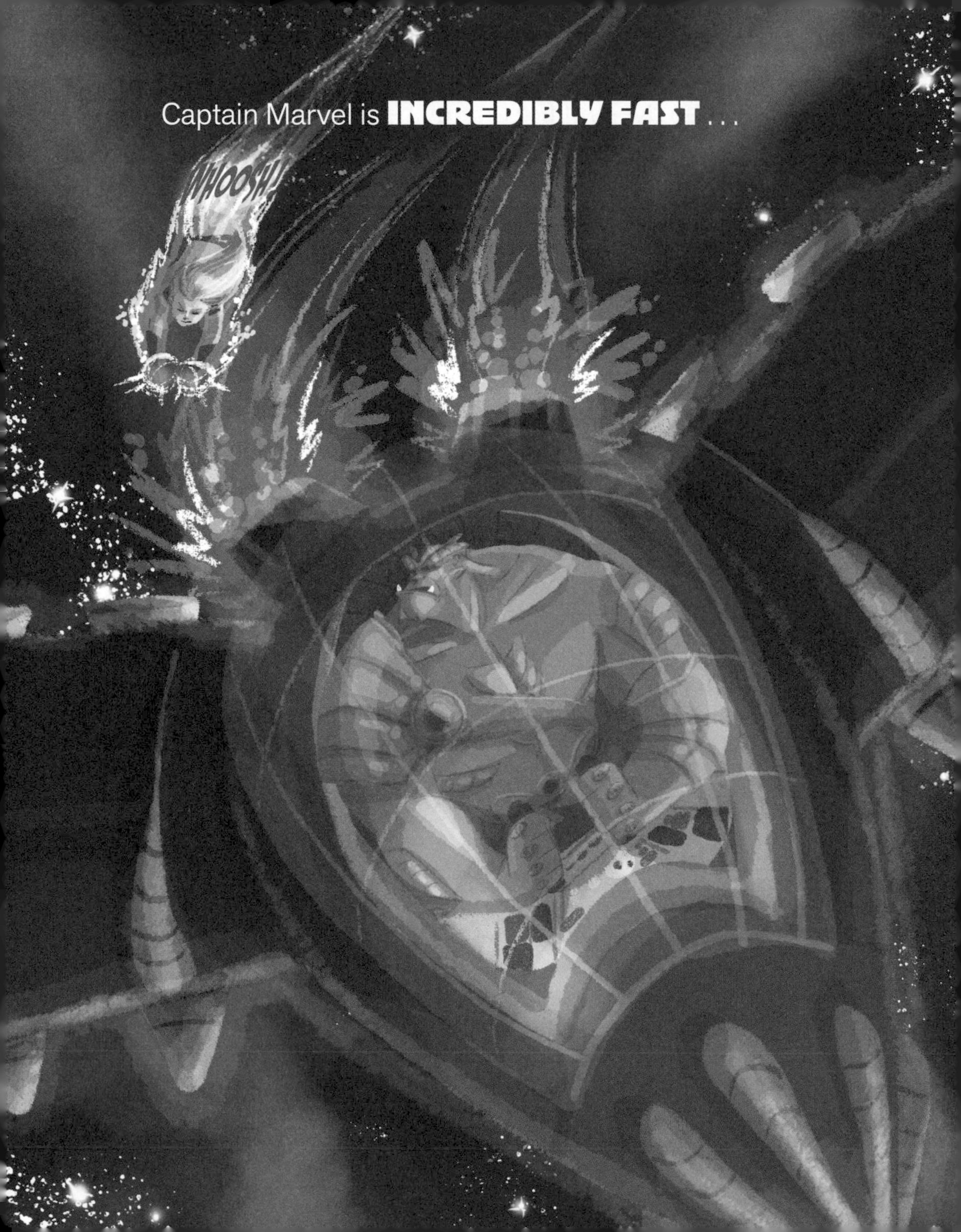
WHOOSH!

. . . and **STRONG**!

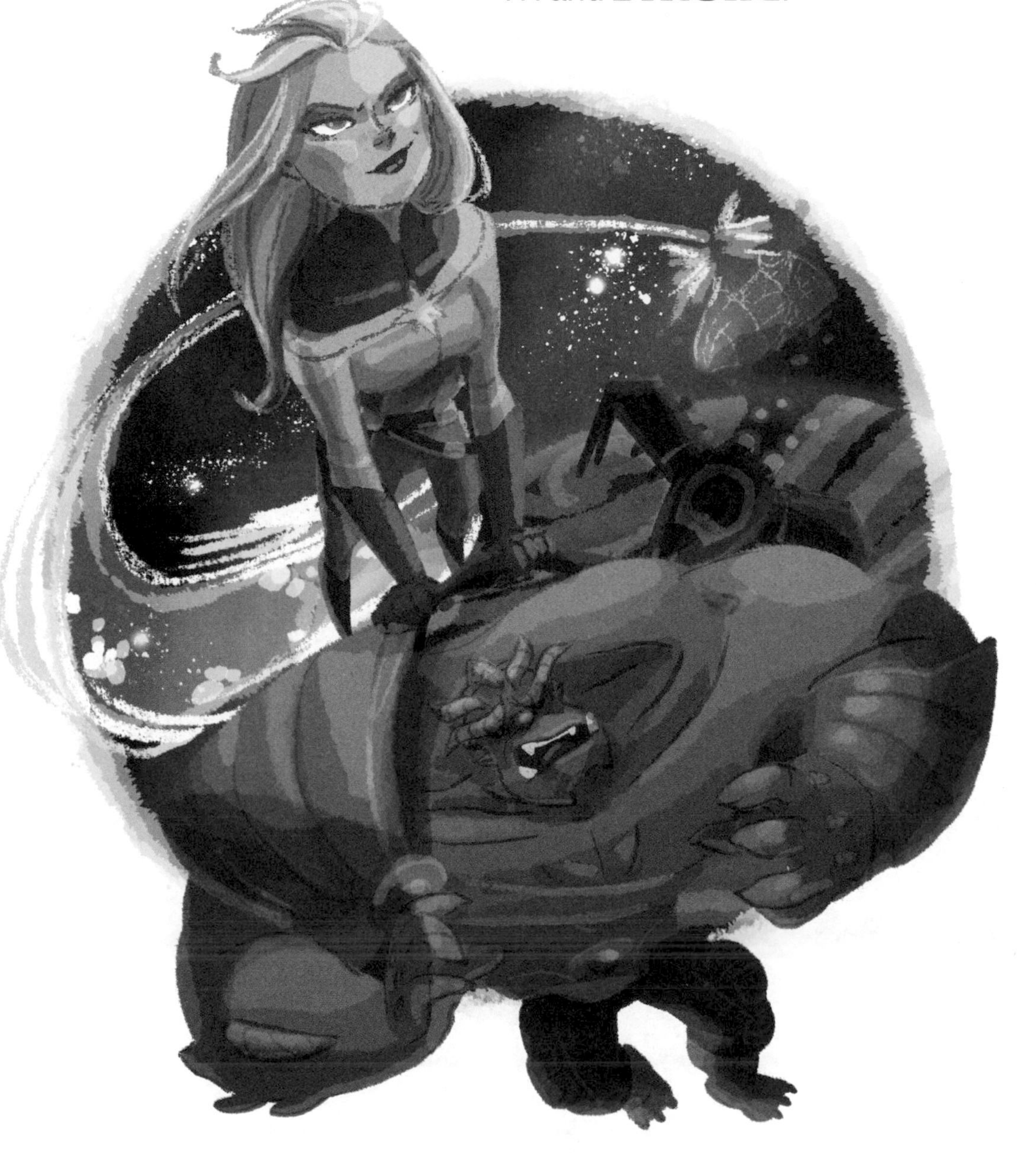

She easily catches intergalactic bad guys . . .

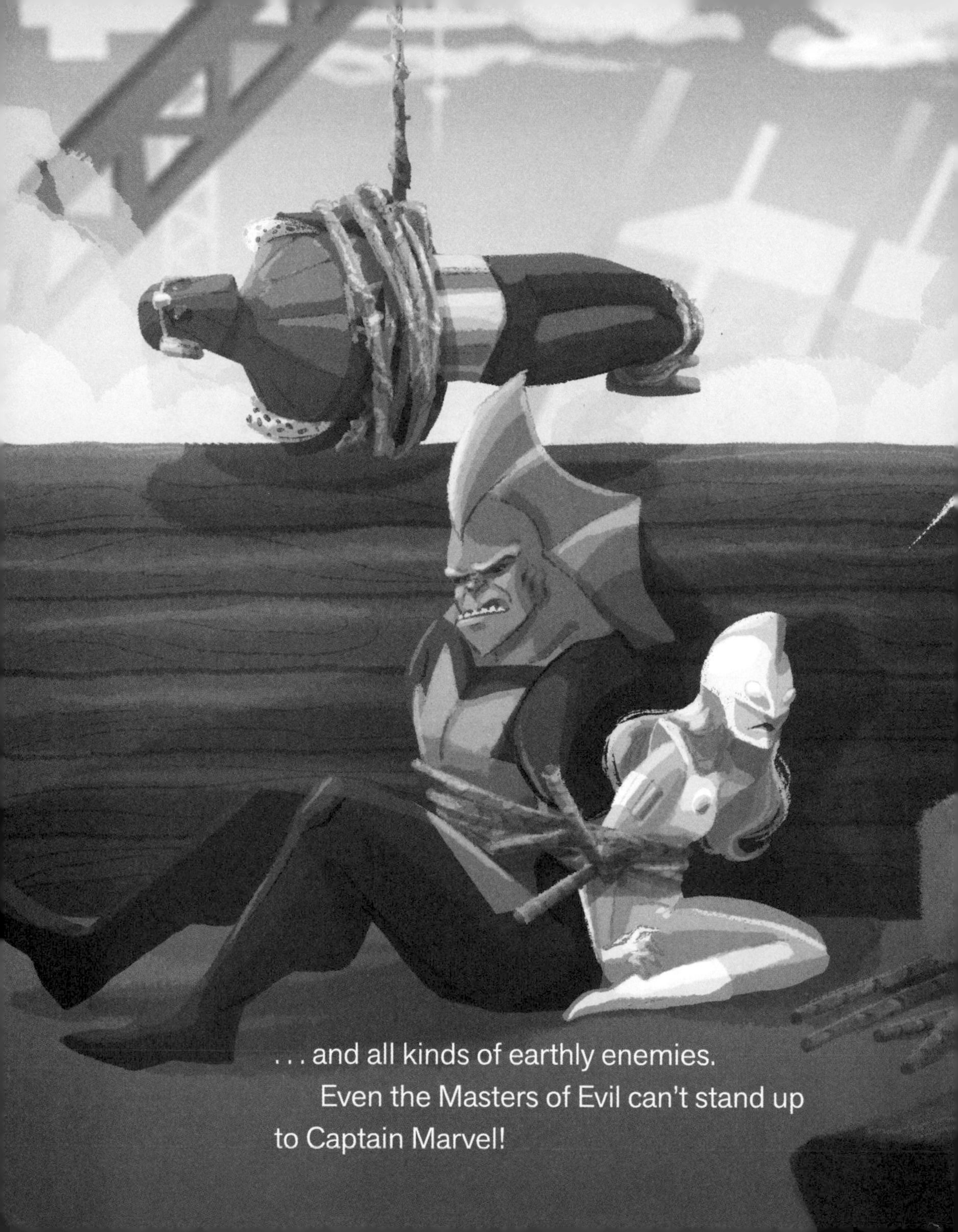

. . . and all kinds of earthly enemies.

Even the Masters of Evil can't stand up to Captain Marvel!

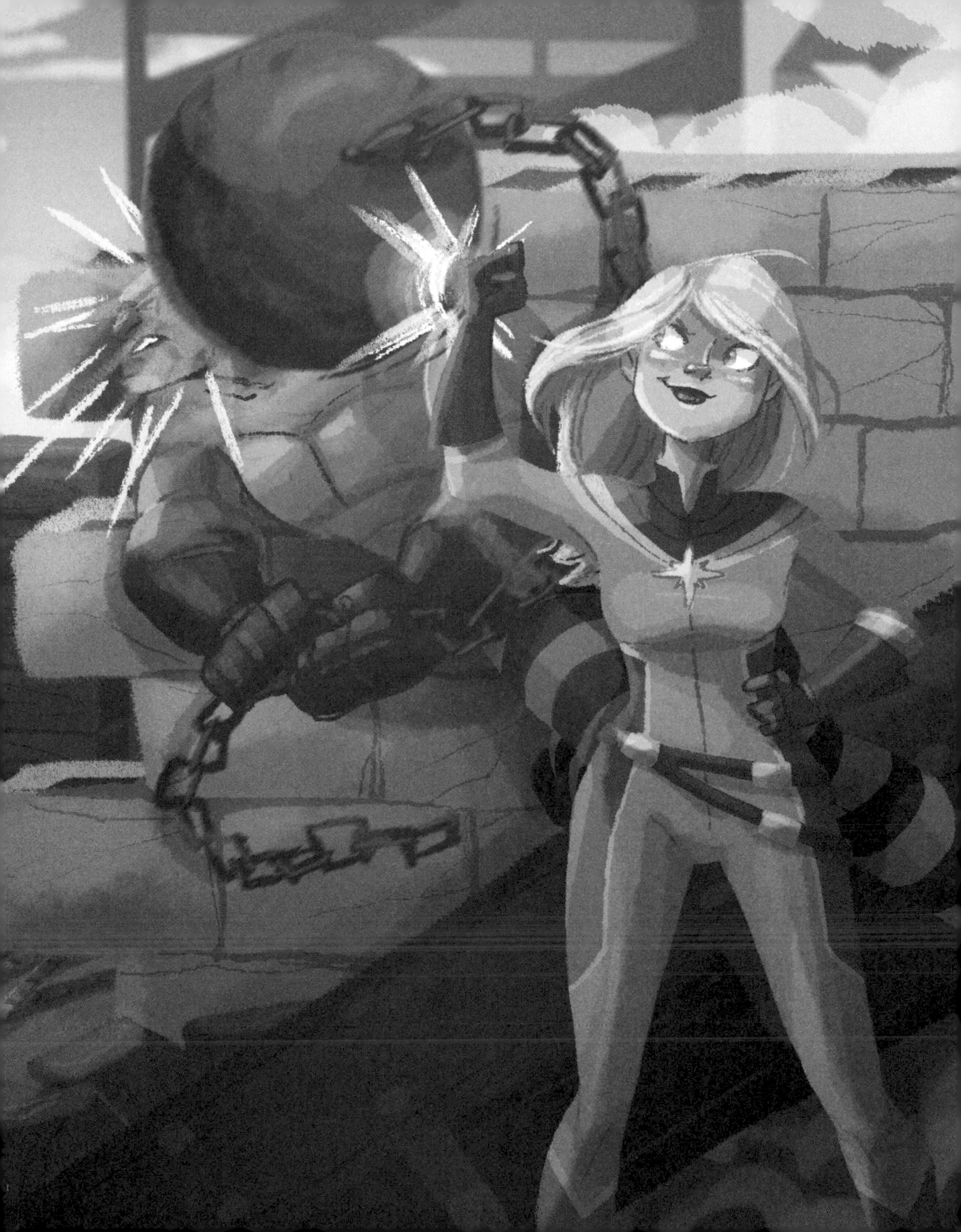

Uh-oh! A kitten is in trouble. Not every rescue Captain Marvel makes involves aliens . . . *or does it?* This ball of fur is really an alien **FLERKEN**.

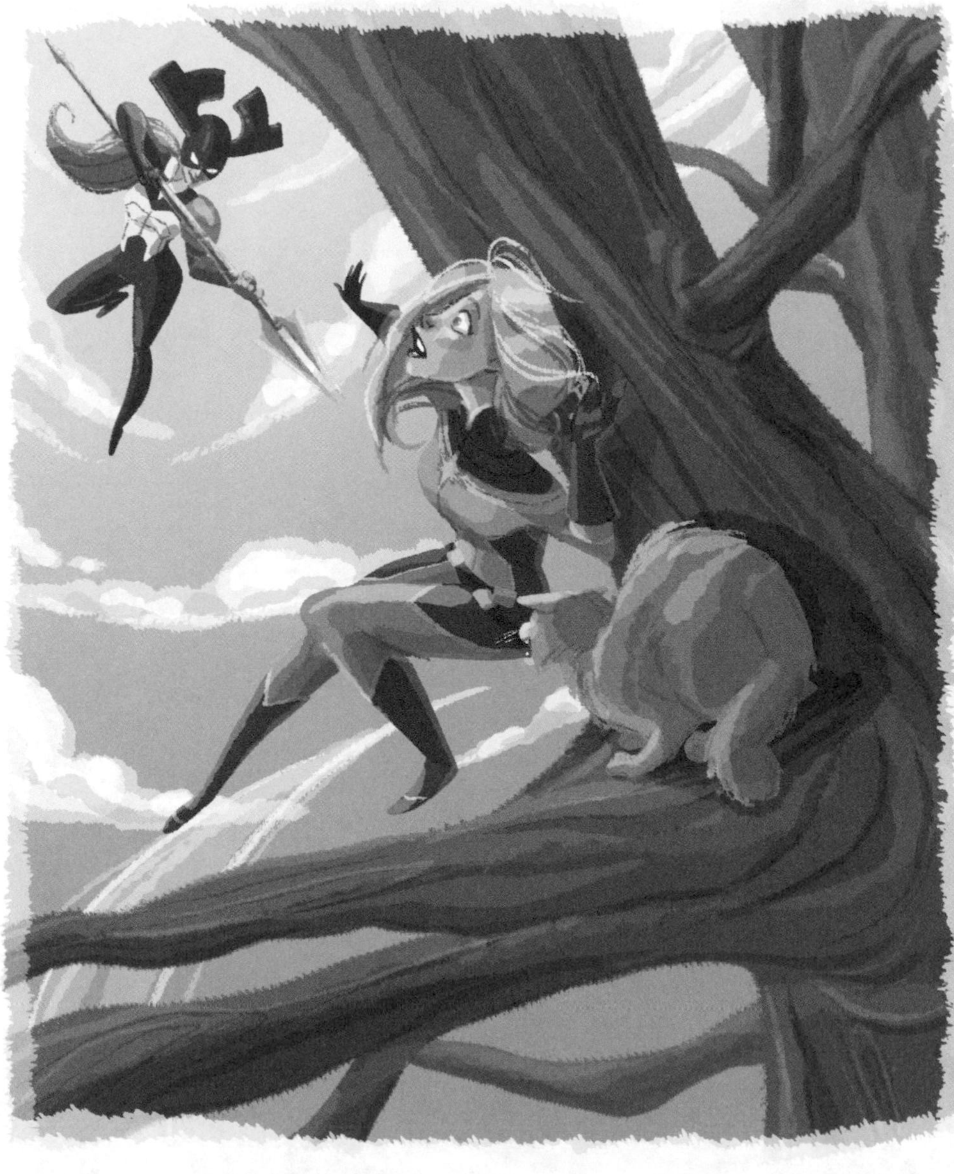

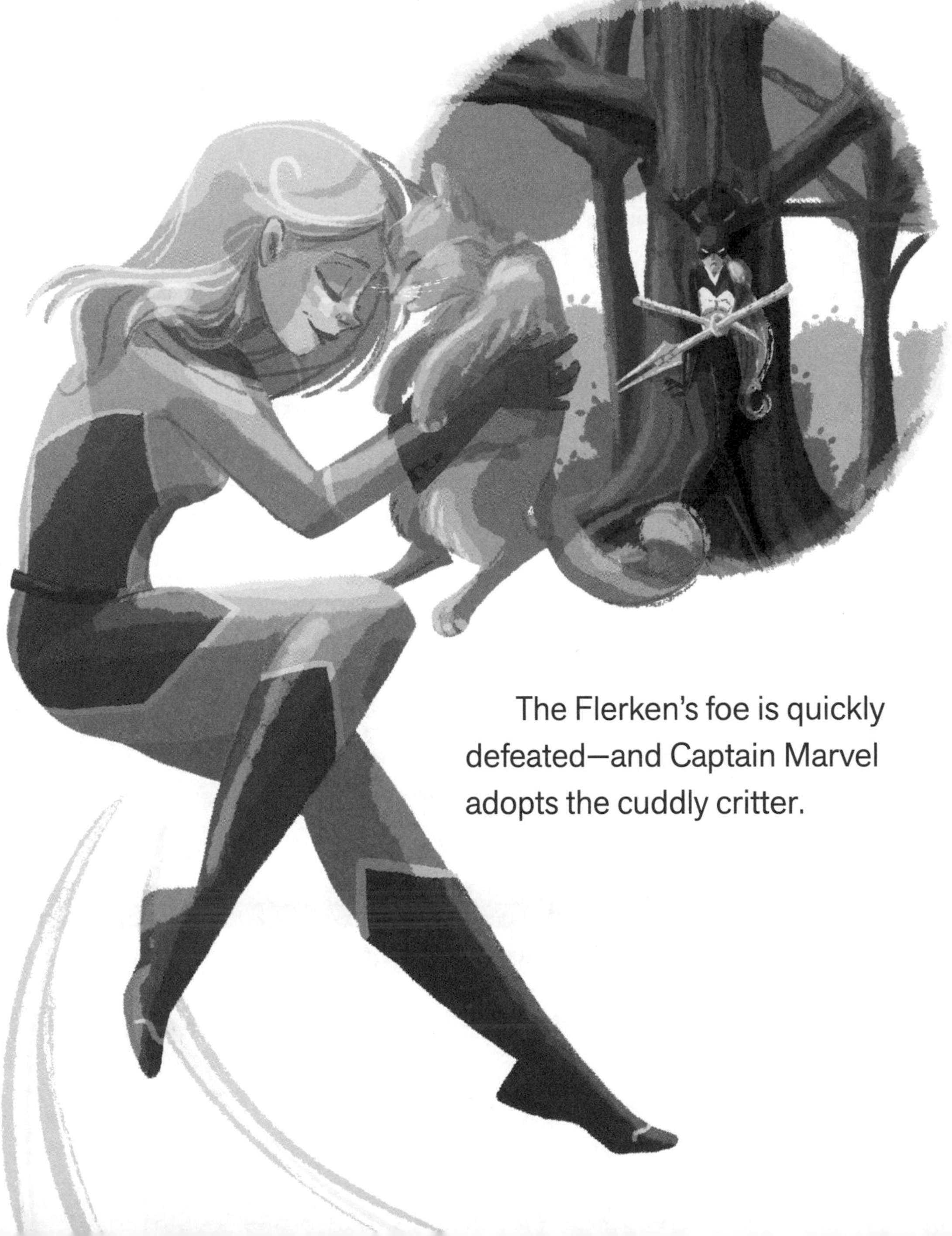

The Flerken's foe is quickly defeated—and Captain Marvel adopts the cuddly critter.

Captain Marvel has another furry friend, **ROCKET RACCOON**. He invites her on cosmic adventures with his buddies, the **GUARDIANS OF THE GALAXY**.

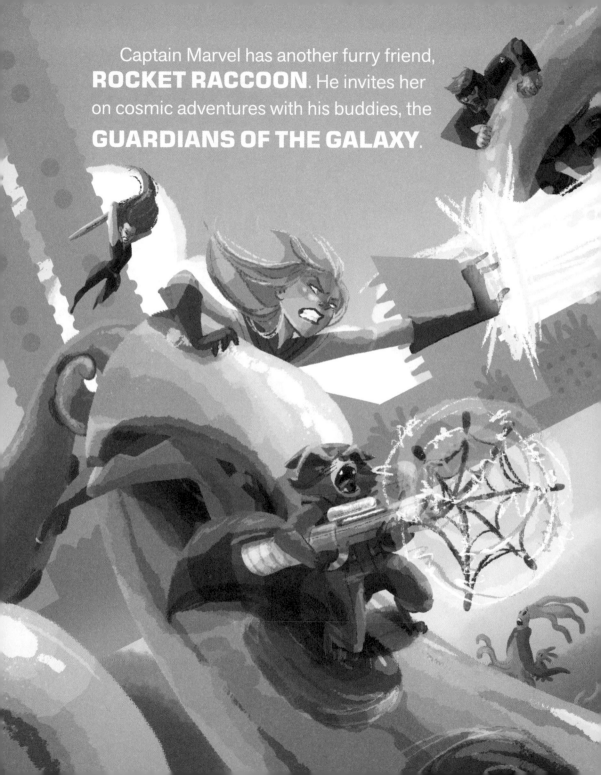

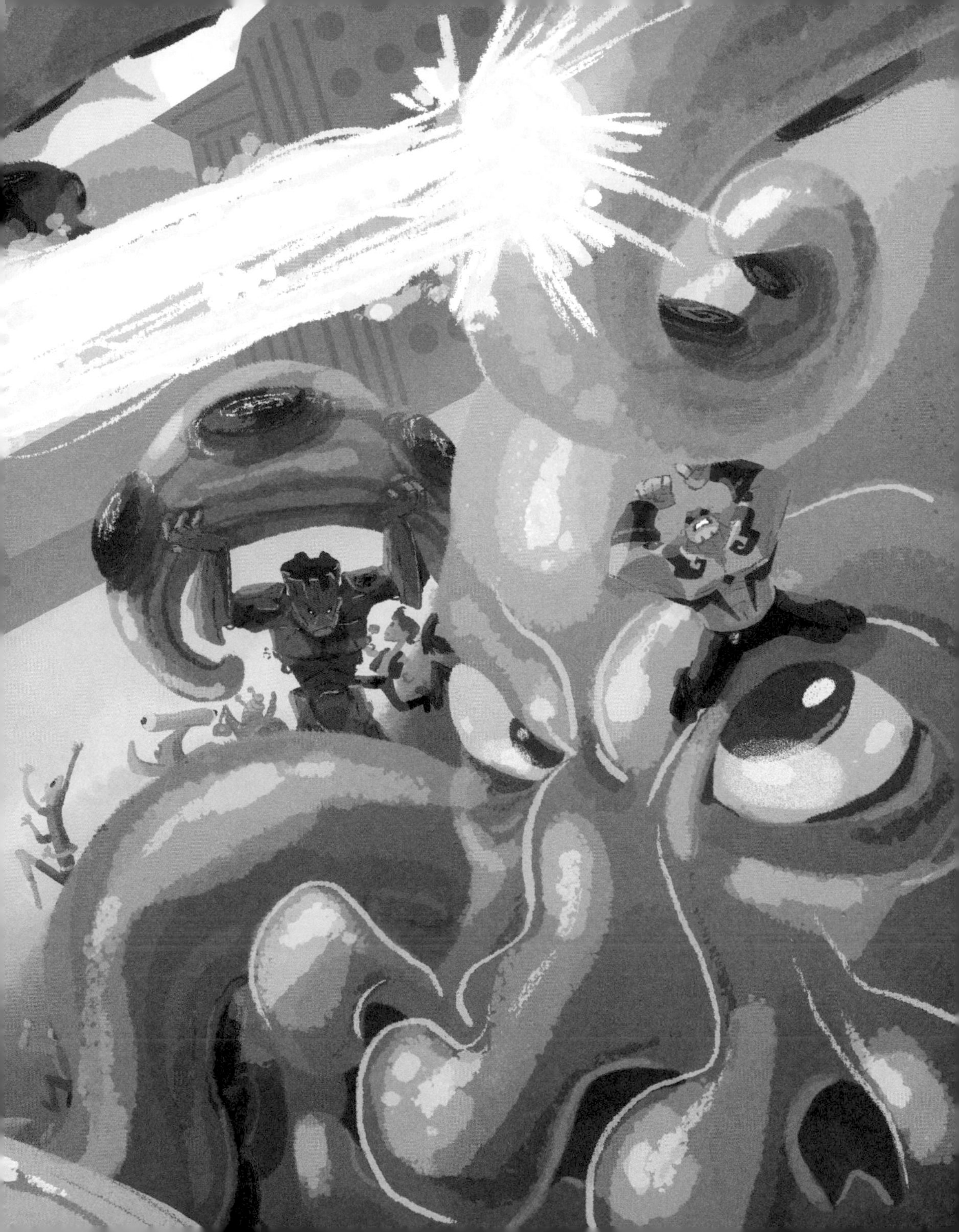

And when alien threats follow her home, Captain Marvel is part of another terrific team—
THE AVENGERS.

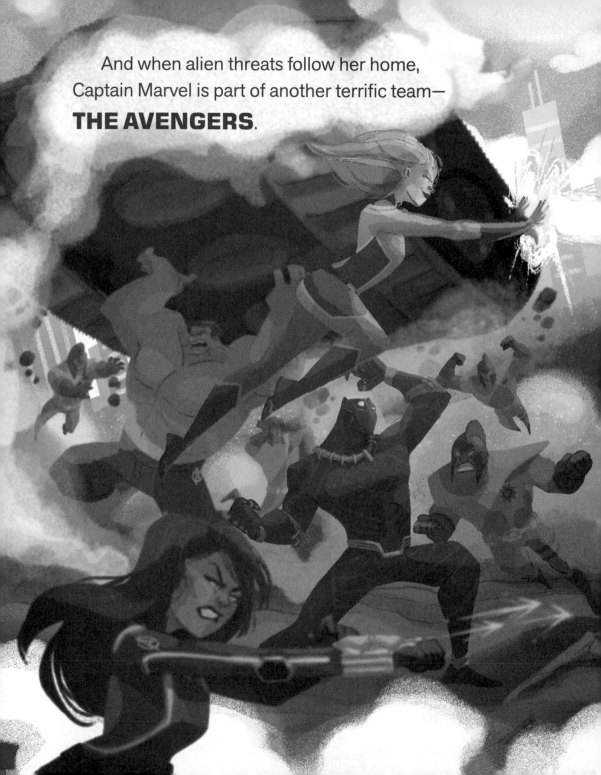

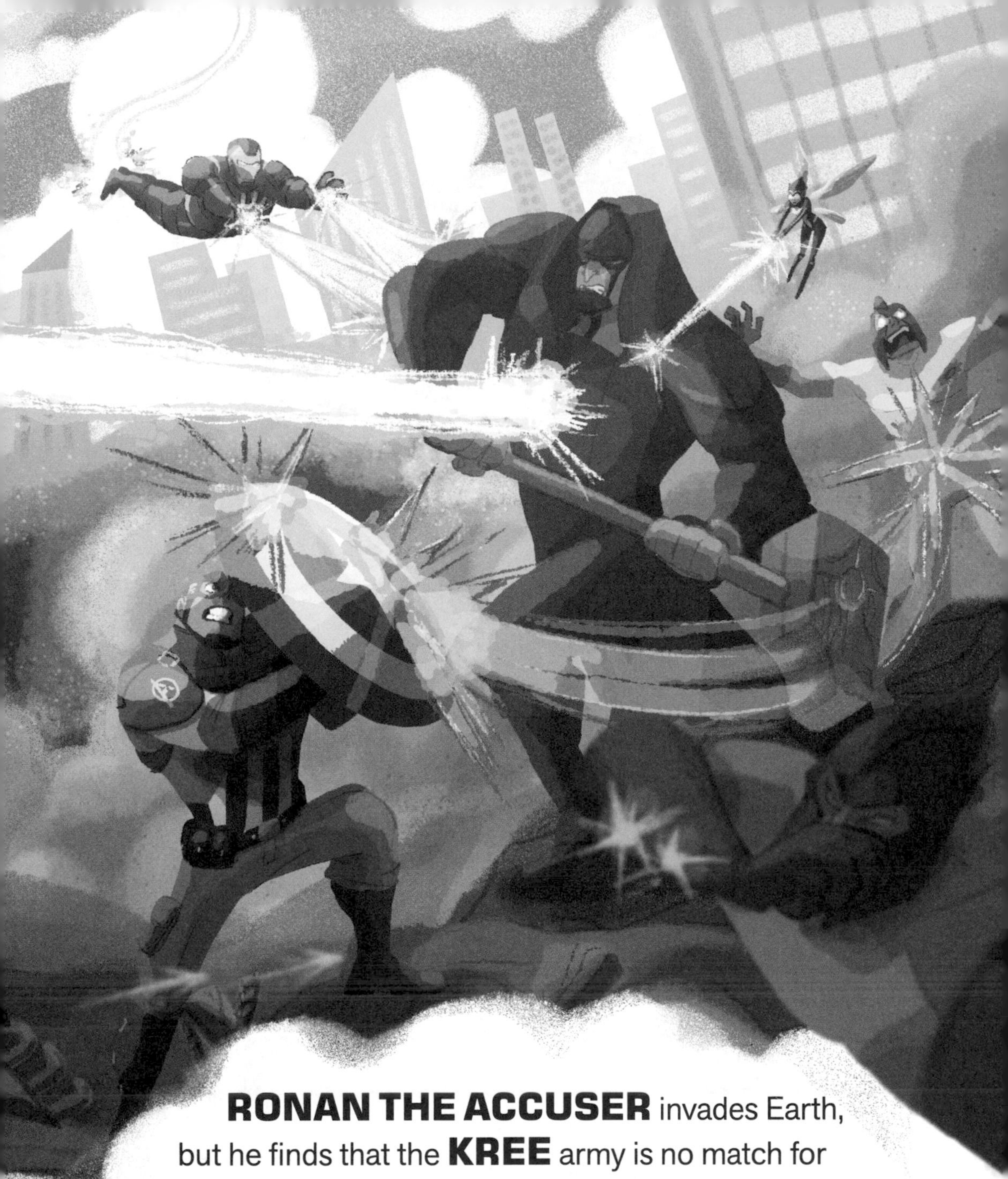

RONAN THE ACCUSER invades Earth, but he finds that the **KREE** army is no match for Captain Marvel and the mighty Avengers.

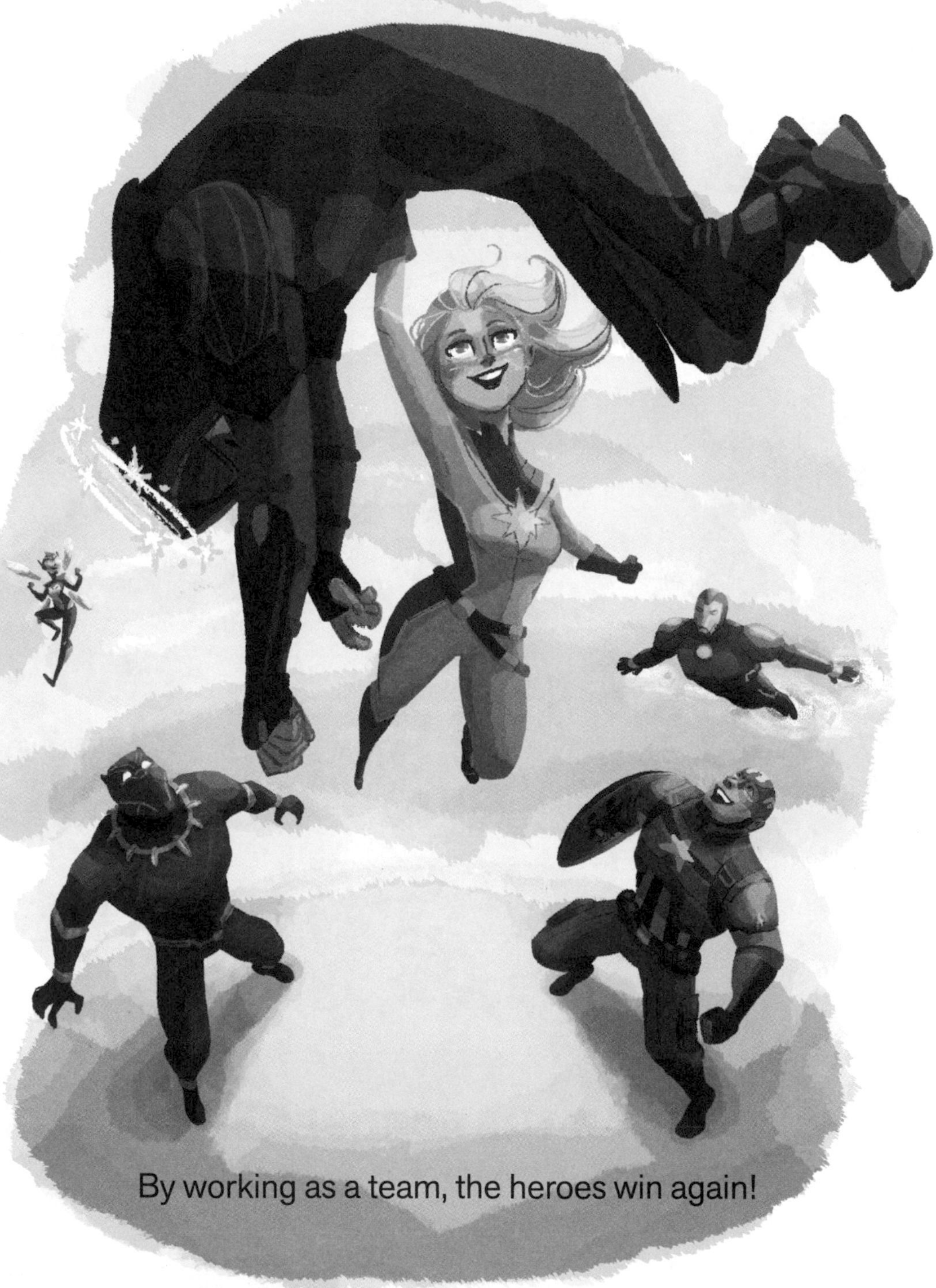

By working as a team, the heroes win again!

Captain Marvel is
an inspiration to people
everywhere . . .

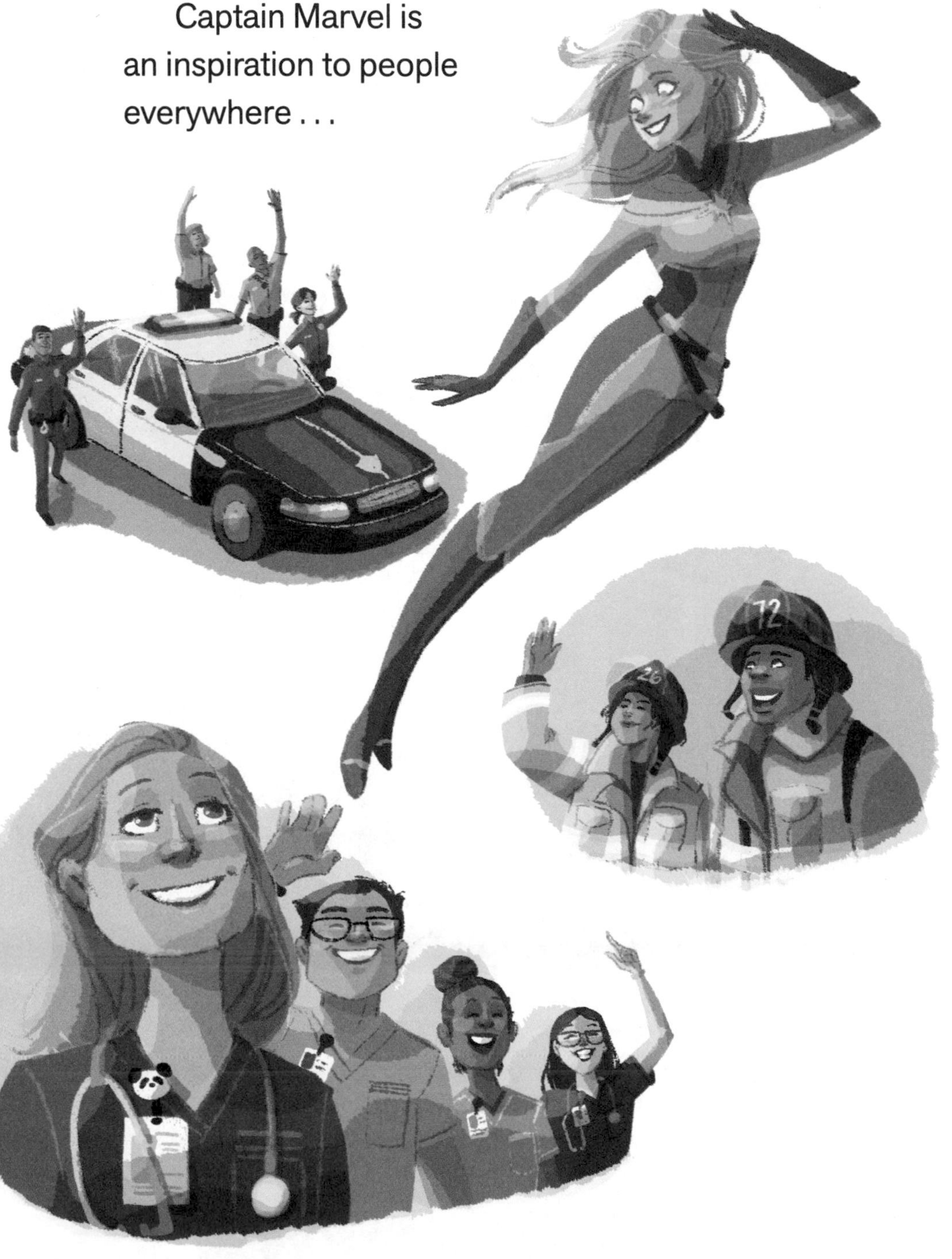
26
72

. . . especially to a girl named **KAMALA KAHN**.

This stretchy, shape-shifting super teen named herself **MS. MARVEL** in honor of her idol.

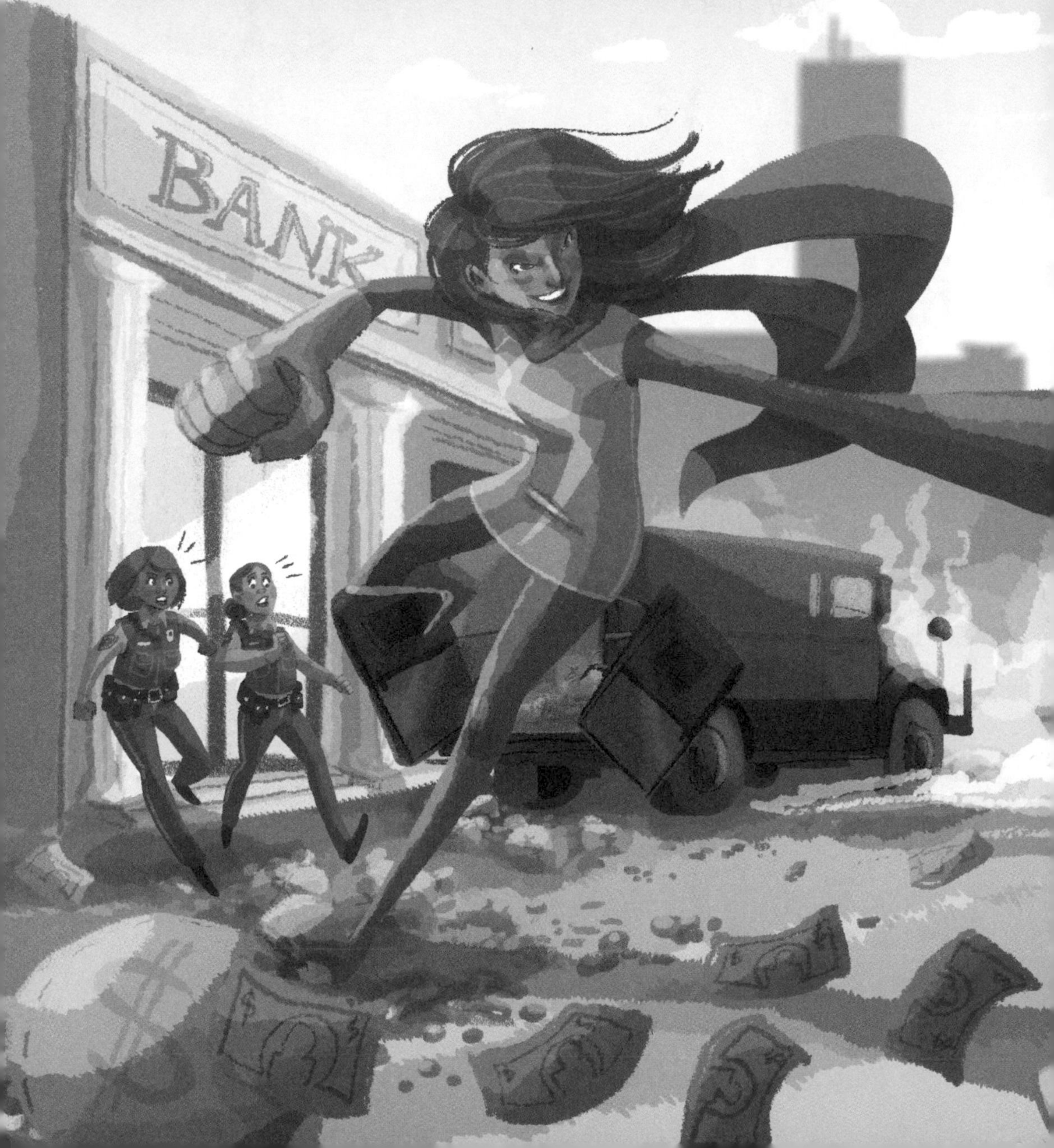
BANK

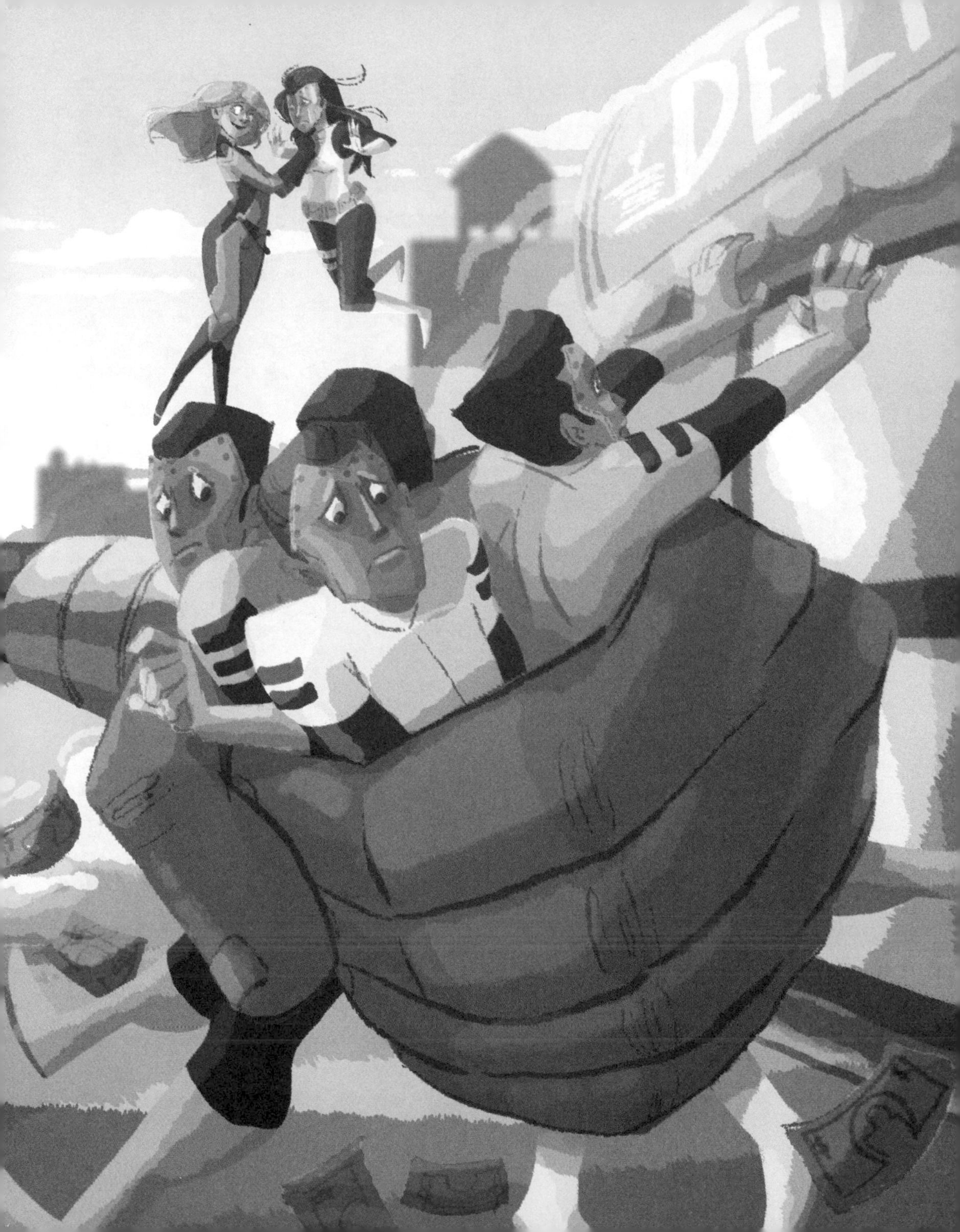
DELI

On Earth or in space, Captain Marvel is a hero who is out of this world.

GO, CAPTAIN MARVEL!

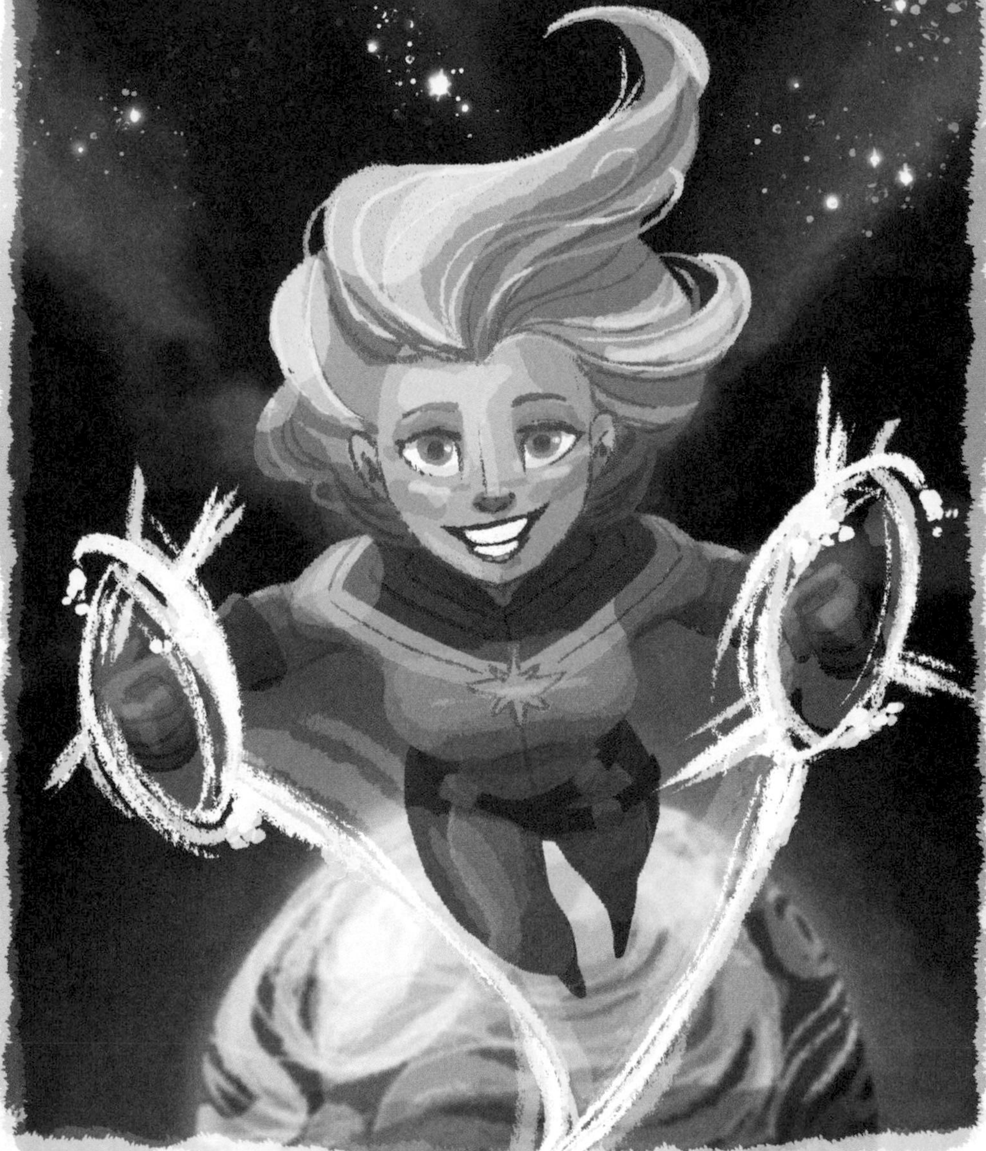